For
Elly Jackson

Special thanks to Michael P. Kambysellis, Professor of Biology, New York University, for his comments on the text and artwork

Text copyright © 1992 by Emery Bernhard   Illustrations copyright © 1992 by Durga Bernhard   All rights reserved   *Printed in the United States of America*   First Edition   Library of Congress Cataloging-in-Publication Data   Bernhard, Emery.   Ladybug / by Emery Bernhard; illustrated by Durga Bernhard.—1st ed.   p. cm.   Summary: Text and pictures introduce the familiar ladybug, consumer of aphids and scale insects and purported carrier of good luck.   ISBN 0-8234-0986-4   1. Ladybugs—Juvenile literature.   [1. Ladybugs.]   I. Bernhard, Durga, ill.   II. Title
QL596.C65B47   1992   92-52714   CIP   AC   595.76′9—dc20

LADYBUG

written by

EMERY BERNHARD

illustrated by

DURGA BERNHARD

Holiday House / New York

I am **not** a lady.
And I am **not** a bug.
I am a . . .

LADYBUG

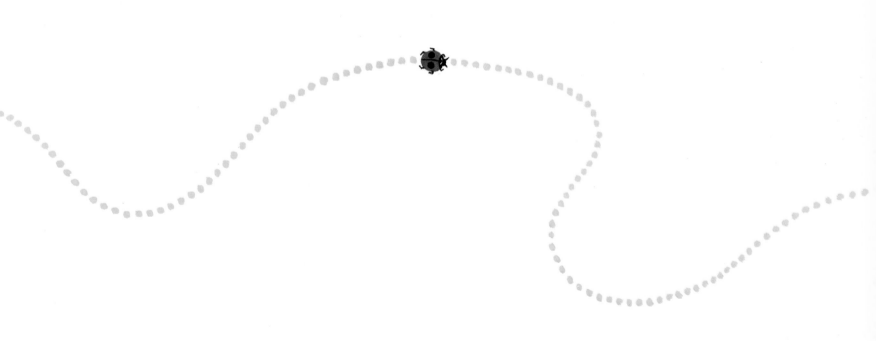

It's the first warm, sunny day of spring on a farm. Winter is barely over, but already the insects are busy.

Ladybugs crawl on alfalfa plants in the pasture. They make their way along the branches of the apple trees.

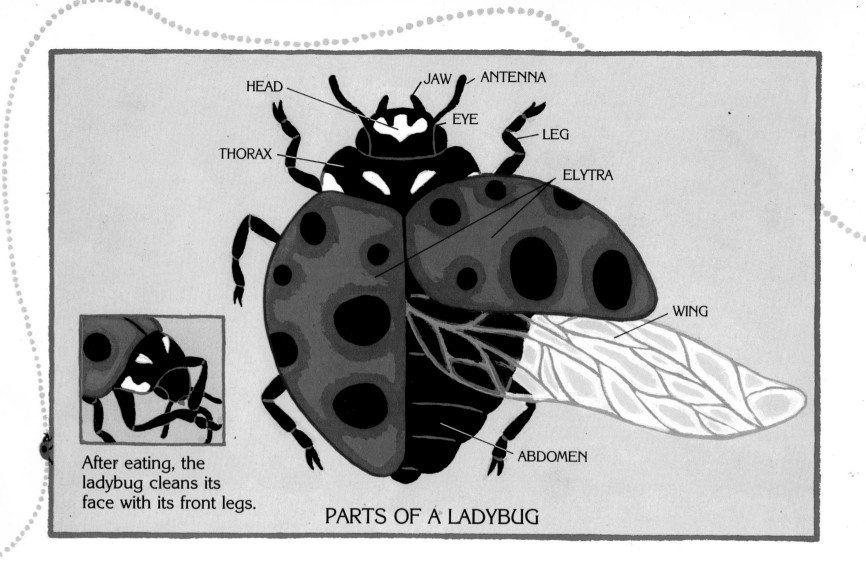

HEAD JAW ANTENNA
EYE
THORAX
LEG
ELYTRA
WING
ABDOMEN

After eating, the ladybug cleans its face with its front legs.

PARTS OF A LADYBUG

A ladybug is a beetle. It has two hard shells, called elytra. They protect the ladybug and cover the hind wings that the ladybug uses for flying.

Ladybugs use their six legs for walking, climbing, and grooming.

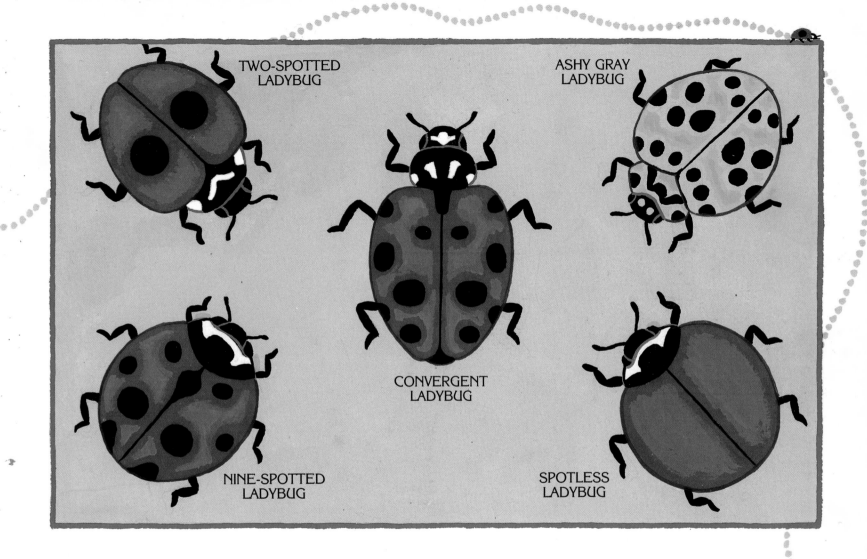

TWO-SPOTTED
LADYBUG

ASHY GRAY
LADYBUG

CONVERGENT
LADYBUG

NINE-SPOTTED
LADYBUG

SPOTLESS
LADYBUG

The ladybug is probably the best known and most popular of all the beetles. Of the 350 kinds of ladybugs in North America, there are five common types.

SCALE INSECTS

Ladybugs have a bad taste, and their shells are quite hard. Most birds and insects do not like to eat them. Some people think the bright colors on the shell warn enemies to keep away.

SCALE
COLONY

APHIDS

Ladybugs have strong jaws. They eat aphids and scale insects—
two kinds of small bugs that are pests in fields and gardens.
Aphids attack many plants, including alfalfa, wheat, and roses.
Scale insects can destroy entire apple and orange orchards.
Gardeners and farmers are happy when they see a ladybug.

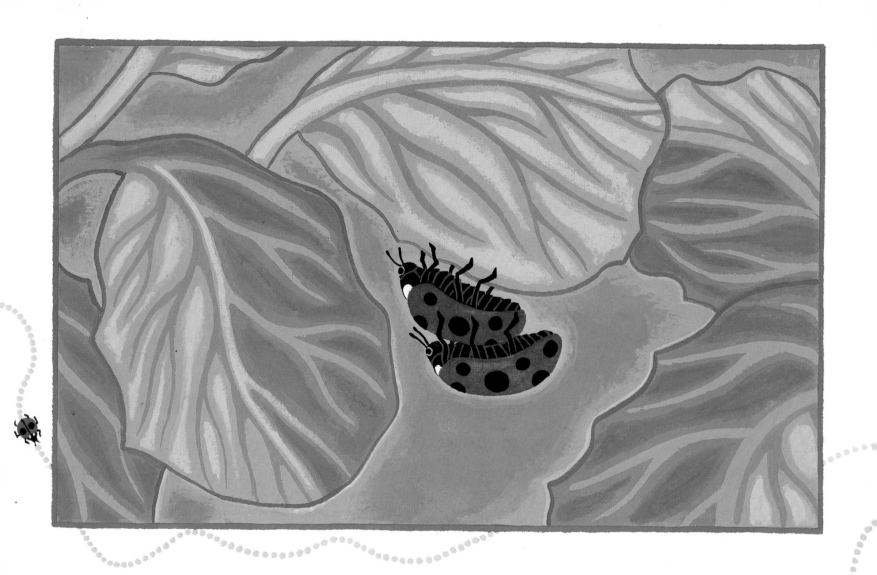

In the spring and summer, the male and female ladybug mate.

After about a week, the female crawls under a leaf. She lays 10 to 100 tiny, gold eggs. The eggs stick to the leaf and are hidden from view.

LARVA

APHIDS

In about five days, the eggs turn white. One breaks open and a pale young ladybug wriggles out. It is called a larva.

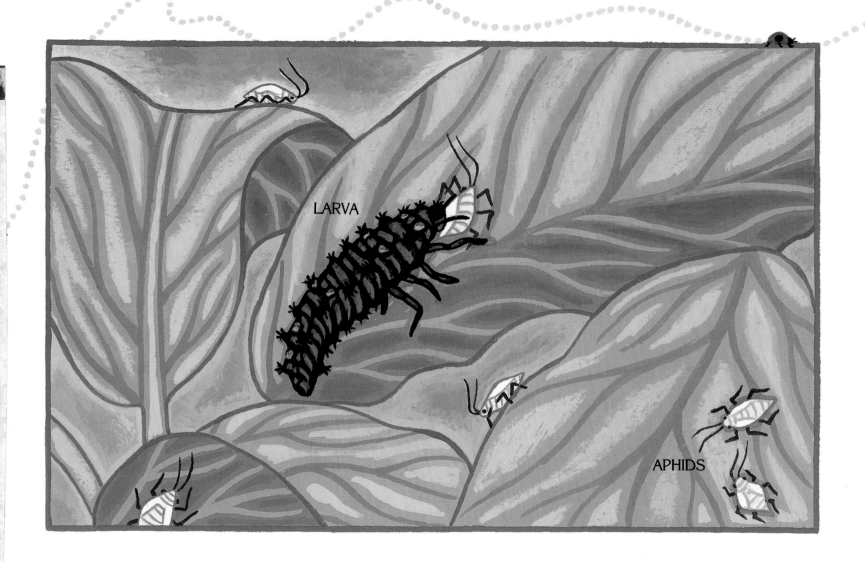

Gradually the bristly larva turns black. For three or four weeks, it eats and grows. In one day, the larva eats about 30 adult aphids.

PUPA

MOLTING

The tough skin of a larva does not stretch. A larva grows larger by shedding its outer skin. This is called molting. The ladybug larva will molt at least three times while feeding and growing. When it is ready to molt for the last time, the larva stops feeding. It cements its tail to a leaf and wriggles out of its outer skin. A new orange skin is waiting underneath. The ladybug is now called a pupa.

For about one week, the pupa stays attached to the leaf. The outside of the pupa hardens into a case. Inside, many changes are taking place. Its body arches and shortens. Its skin thickens. Wings sprout. Finally full-grown, the adult beetle pushes its head out of its case and wriggles free. The new ladybug is soft and gold. As its shell dries and hardens, it turns red and spots appear.

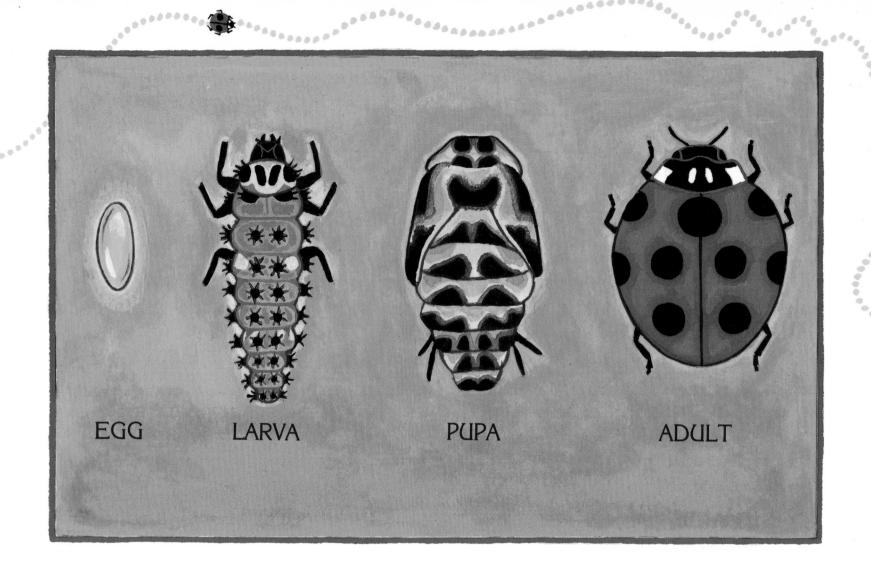

EGG   LARVA   PUPA   ADULT

The ladybug has changed from larva to pupa to adult. This is called metamorphosis. Ladybug metamorphosis takes three weeks in warm weather and as long as six weeks in cold.

The ladybug takes to the air for the first time, raising its outer shells to uncover its new wings.

When there is a shortage of aphids and scale insects, the ladybug travels in search of food. Ladybugs are slow and clumsy fliers. Often they crawl on their short legs instead of flying.

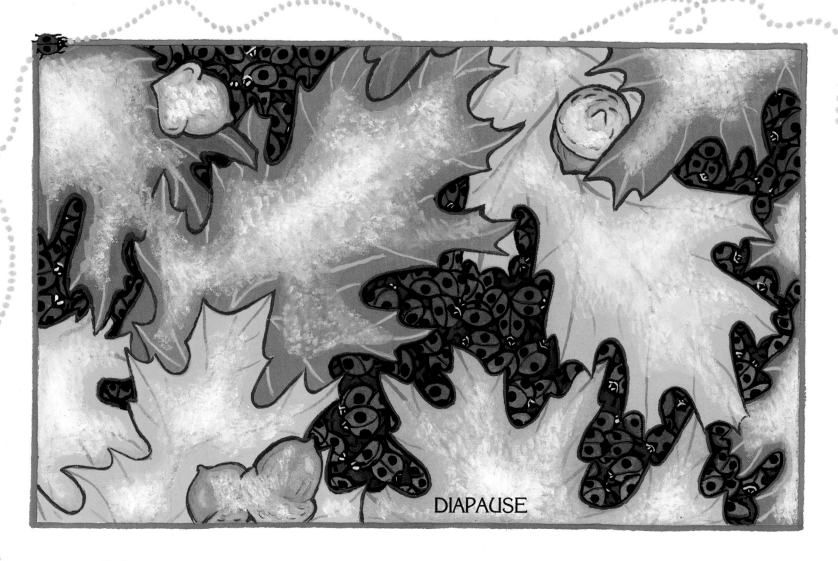

DIAPAUSE

Like many animals, ladybugs look for shelter before cold
weather sets in. During the winter, ladybugs rest quietly. This is
called diapause. They often huddle together in the thousands
under leaves, bark, rocks, and porches. In early spring, they
begin searching for food again.

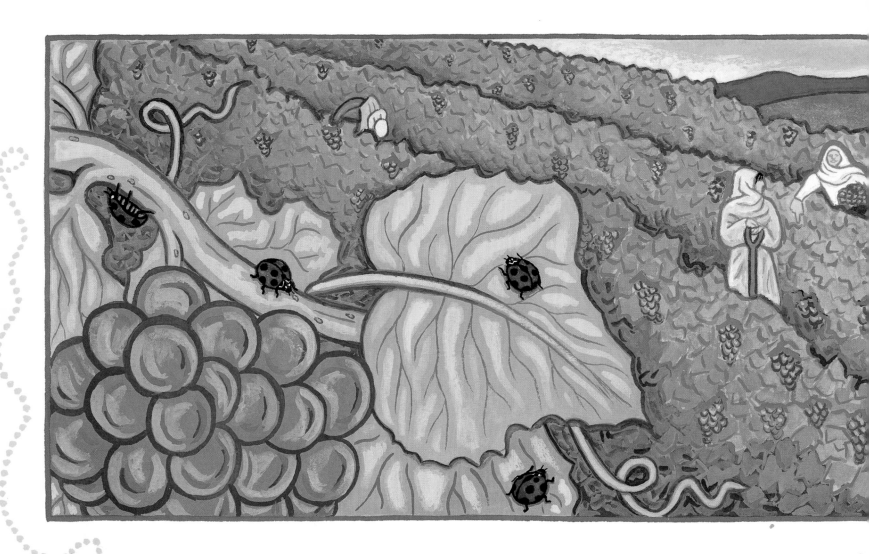

For at least 1,500 years, farmers in Europe have welcomed ladybugs on their vines, knowing that ladybugs eat insect pests.

Feeling thankful to these brightly colored beetles—and grateful to the Mother of Jesus who they worshipped—people in the Middle ages called ladybugs Beetles of Our Blessed Lady.

In England, ladybugs are called ladybirds. Long ago, when farmers burned their vines after the harvest, they said a special rhyme to send the beetles away from the fire.

Ladybird, ladybird, fly away home!
Your house is on fire,
your children all gone,
All but one, and her name is Ann,
And she crept under the pudding pan.

In time this rhyme found its way into the Mother Goose collection of nursery rhymes, first published in about 1760. We don't know if saying the old rhyme saved any ladybugs. We do know that ladybugs have saved many plants.

People once thought that ladybugs had magical powers. In Europe, if a girl wanted a boyfriend, she would let a ladybug perch on the tips of her fingers. She would tell it to "fly away home" and then let it go. She believed her boyfriend would come from wherever the ladybug flew.

Ladybugs have been used in the orange groves of California since 1888. It takes about 3,000 ladybugs to protect an acre of trees. When orange growers tried using pesticide to get rid of fruit pests, the poison also killed ladybugs. Scale insects began to cover the orange trees. Then millions of ladybugs were shipped to the orange groves to feast on the scales. The trees were saved.

Today, farmers and gardeners order ladybugs from ladybug breeders who send them by mail. The ladybugs are set free near the plants that need protection from insect pests.

In early America, it was said that a ladybug would bring good luck if it was found in the house in winter. It is still good luck, and now we know why!

Glossary

abdomen (AB-doh-men): The rear section of an insect's body.

alfalfa (al-FAHL-fah): A leafy plant grown in fields and pastures to feed animals and nourish the soil.

aphids (A-fids): Small insects with soft bodies that suck the juice of plants.

beetle: An insect with four wings. The two outer wings are hard and cover the two soft inner wings.

breeder: A person who raises animals or plants.

bug: A common name for many insects, but a true bug has sucking mouthparts.

diapause (DIE-ah-pawz): A period of time when an insect is inactive.

elytra (eh-LIE-truh): A beetle's hard outer wings that cover the soft inner wings.

insect (IN-sekt): A small animal with three main body parts, three pairs of legs, and usually one or two pairs of wings.

ladybirds: The name for ladybugs in Great Britain.

larva: An insect in the second stage of metamorphosis, in which it has no wings and looks like a worm.

metamorphosis (met-uh-MOR-fuh-sis): The changes in an insect that take place from the larval to pupal to adult stages.

molt: To shed the outer covering (of an animal's body).

pest: An insect that is destructive to the plants that people grow.

pesticide (PEST-ih-side): A chemical used to destroy pests; it may also harm other animals.

pupa (PEW-puh): An insect in the third stage of metamorphosis, in which the larva changes into an adult insect.

scale insects: Small sucking insects that attach themselves to plants.

thorax (THOR-ax): The middle section of an insect's body, to which two pairs of wings and three pairs of legs are attached.